SANTA'S DRAGON

Santa's Dragon

Copyright © 2021 by Sky Railway LLC
Published 2021 by Sky Railway Publishing Co.
P.O. Box 4188
Santa Fe, NM 87502
skyrailway.com
Sky Railway Publishing Co. is owned by Sky Railway LLC, which operates adventure and Christmas train excursions on the historic spur line between Santa Fe and Lamy, New Mexico. To learn more about Sky Railway adventures or the Christmas train and reserve tickets, please visit our website at skyrailway.com.

Cover image and illustrations: Raya Golden
Interior formatting: E.M. Tippetts Book Designs

Santa's Dragon is a work of fiction. Any resemblance to actual events, places, incidents, or persons, living or dead, is entirely coincidental.

ISBN: 978-1-7375512-0-1
Printed in the United States of America
First United States Edition
First Printing, September 2021

This is the story of the last two dragons
in New Mexico.

One was a good dragon, and he had the regal name of Pablo el Dragón Morado de Fuego y Humo, which in English is Pablo the Purple Dragon of Fire and Smoke. He called himself Pablito for short.

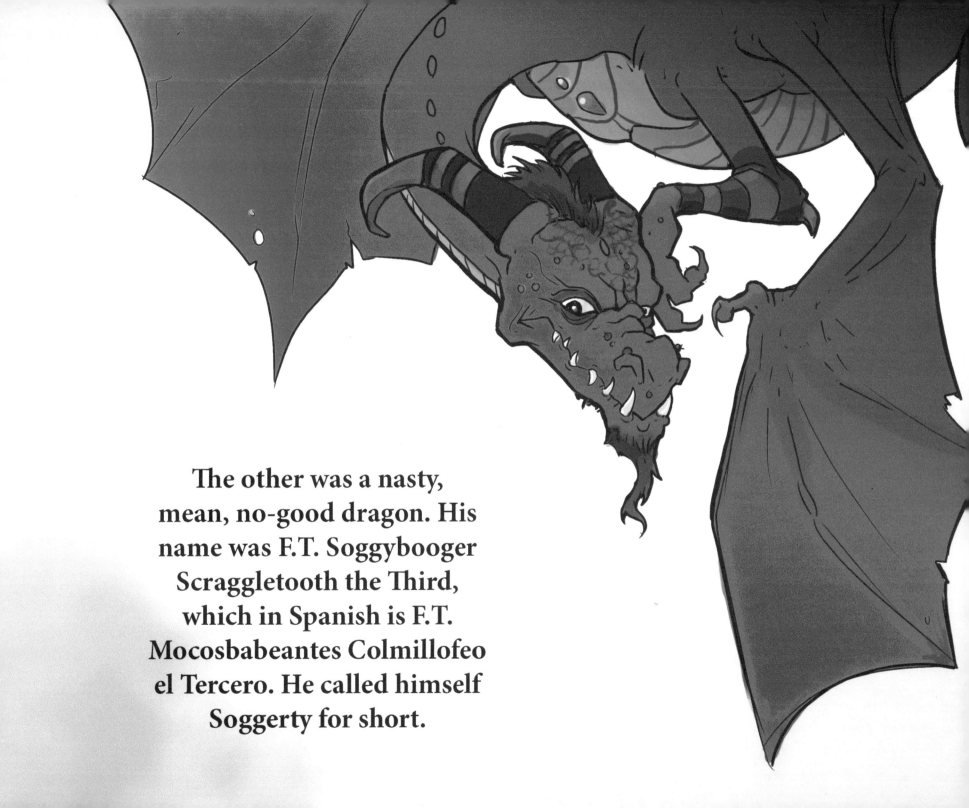

The other was a nasty, mean, no-good dragon. His name was F.T. Soggybooger Scraggletooth the Third, which in Spanish is F.T. Mocosbabeantes Colmillofeo el Tercero. He called himself Soggerty for short.

Pablito was a lonely dragon. Long ago, when most of the dragons in the world mysteriously disappeared, Pablito's friends and family vanished with them. He hadn't seen another nice dragon in many years. Dragons like to travel together, just like herds of horses or flocks of birds. A group of dragons together is called a thunder of dragons.

But Pablito had no friends.
He was a thunder of one.

All year, Pablito longed for company, but as Christmas approached, he felt especially lonely.

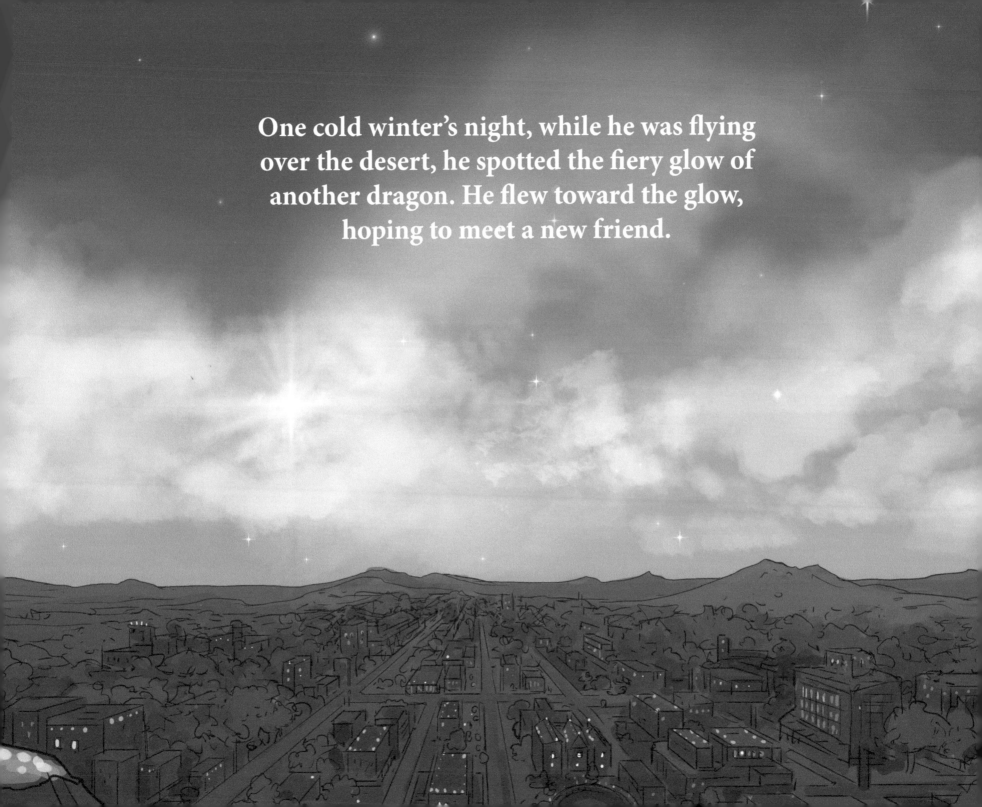

One cold winter's night, while he was flying over the desert, he spotted the fiery glow of another dragon. He flew toward the glow, hoping to meet a new friend.

But when he got closer, his heart sank. It was not a new friend at all. It was the greedy old dragon Soggerty.

But why was he flying so fast
toward the town of Santa Fe?

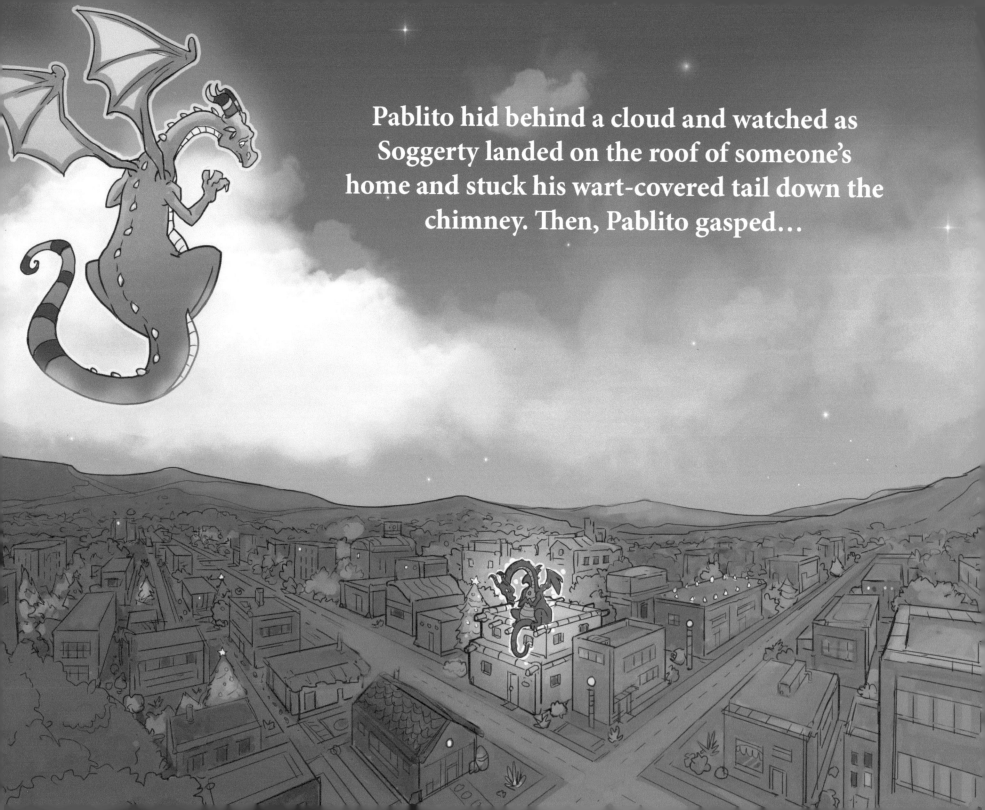

Pablito hid behind a cloud and watched as Soggerty landed on the roof of someone's home and stuck his wart-covered tail down the chimney. Then, Pablito gasped…

That mean old dragon was stealing Christmas presents! Soggerty went from house to house with his ugly, thieving tail, taking Christmas presents left for children by Santa.

When Soggerty was finished, he flew away. Pablito quietly shadowed Soggerty all the way to his cave high up in the black cliffs of Diablo Canyon and watched him slither into his lair with the children's presents.

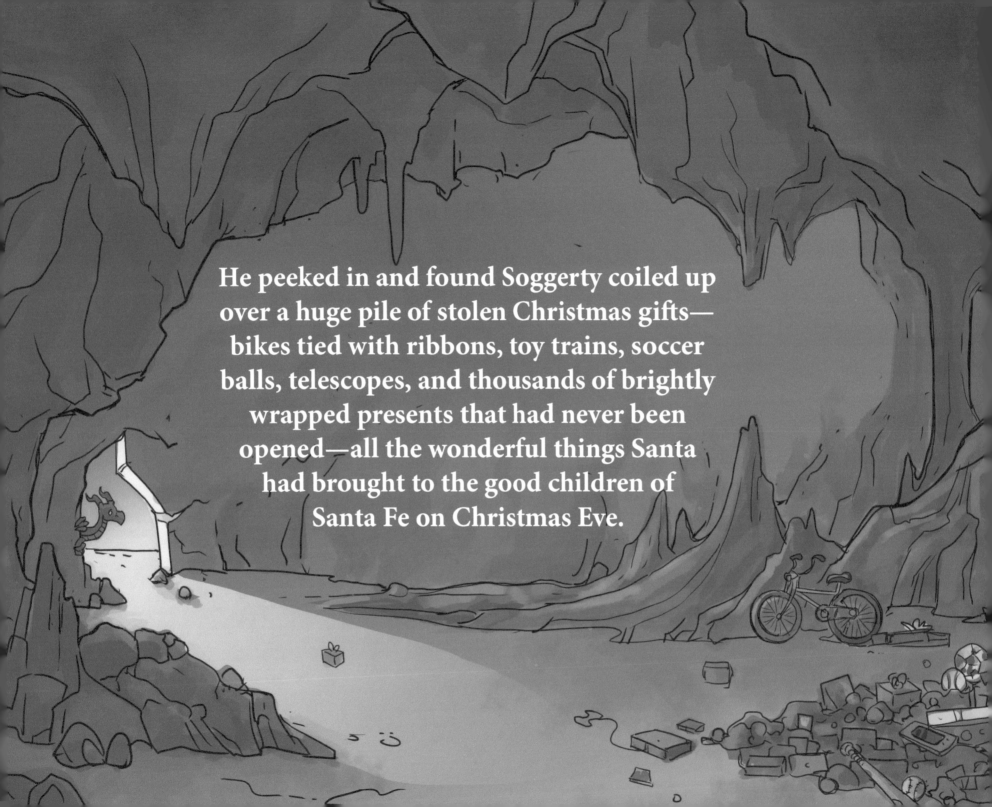

He peeked in and found Soggerty coiled up over a huge pile of stolen Christmas gifts— bikes tied with ribbons, toy trains, soccer balls, telescopes, and thousands of brightly wrapped presents that had never been opened—all the wonderful things Santa had brought to the good children of Santa Fe on Christmas Eve.

"Soggerty!" cried Pablito. "You've been stealing Christmas presents!" Pablito stormed into the cave. "Some of these presents were supposed to go to children so long ago, they're all grown up now!"

Soggerty just coiled up tighter around the pile of glittering toys and hissed, "They're mine, all mine!"

"No, they aren't," said Pablito. "This is terrible! You've been stealing Christmas presents from kids all these years? You're a mean, selfish dragon! These are for people. They're not for dragons. Dragons can't ride a bike or play soccer!"

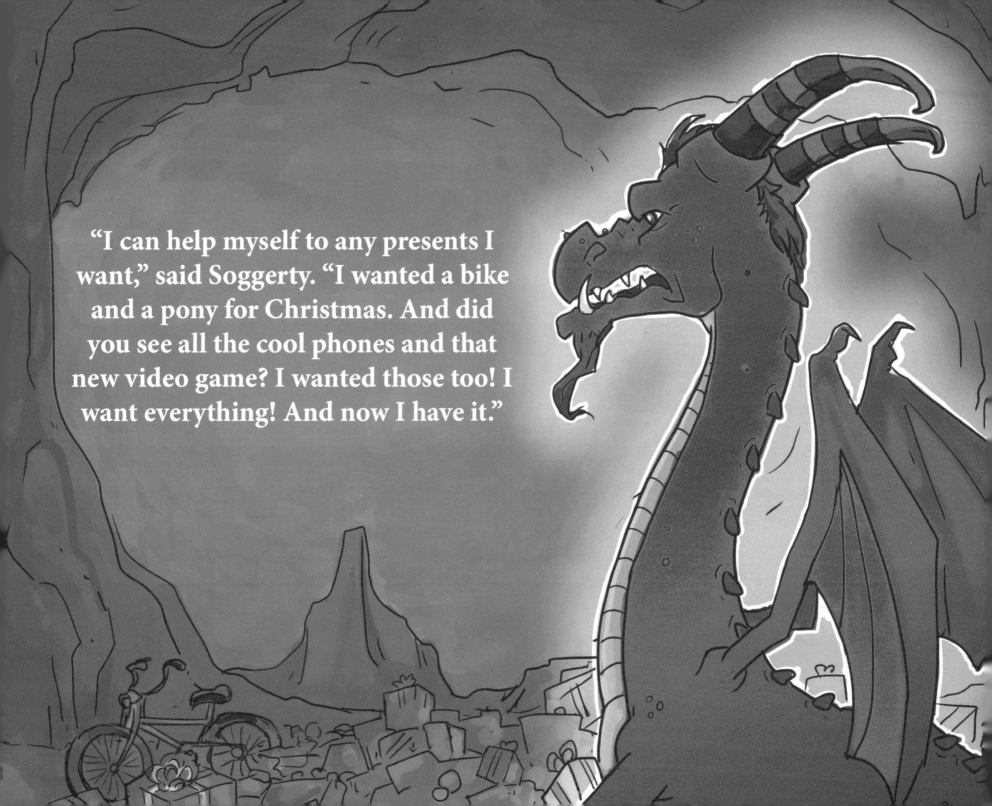

"I can help myself to any presents I want," said Soggerty. "I wanted a bike and a pony for Christmas. And did you see all the cool phones and that new video game? I wanted those too! I want everything! And now I have it."

"If you don't leave me alone, I'm going to breathe fire and smoke all over you," Soggerty said grumpily.

Pablito laughed. "I'm a dragon too, you silly old grouch. I love fire and smoke. So go ahead!"

Soggerty stood and huffed fire and puffed smoke all over Pablito. But Pablito just wrinkled his nose because Soggerty's breath stank like old cheese!

Then Pablito let out a huge blast of fire so hot, it pushed back Soggerty's flames and singed off some of his warts.

When Soggerty saw Pablito standing up to him for the children,
like all bullies he backed down.

"Ouch, ouch! Stop! Don't hurt my beautiful warts!
Take this stuff and leave me alone!"

"I will," said Pablito. "And don't ever steal Christmas presents again!"

And so, Pablito carefully loaded up the toys
and presents from Soggerty's cave and
flew toward Santa Fe to give them
back to all the boys and girls.

On his way, he spied another flying light
in the sky, glowing soft and red.
"Oh no!" he said. "Not Soggerty again!"
But it wasn't Soggerty this time…

It was Santa in his sleigh, pulled by his trusty reindeer! Santa flew up alongside Pablito and said, "Pablito, I'm so proud of the way you stood up to that nasty dragon and saved all these presents for the children. You are carrying a lot of toys! Do you need help taking them back to the girls and boys of Santa Fe?"

"I sure do," said Pablito. "Being a dragon, I might scare the children when I deliver their presents."

"Aha!" cried Santa. "I have an idea! I can magically change you into a Christmas train to deliver the presents in Santa Fe. What do you think, Pablito?"

"That's an amazing idea!" said Pablito. "I've always wanted to ride a train."
Santa smiled. "And now you can be one! Just for Christmas Eve, of course."

And with a wave of his hand, Santa changed Pablo the Purple Dragon into a bright, beautiful train filled with presents for all the boys and girls of Santa Fe.

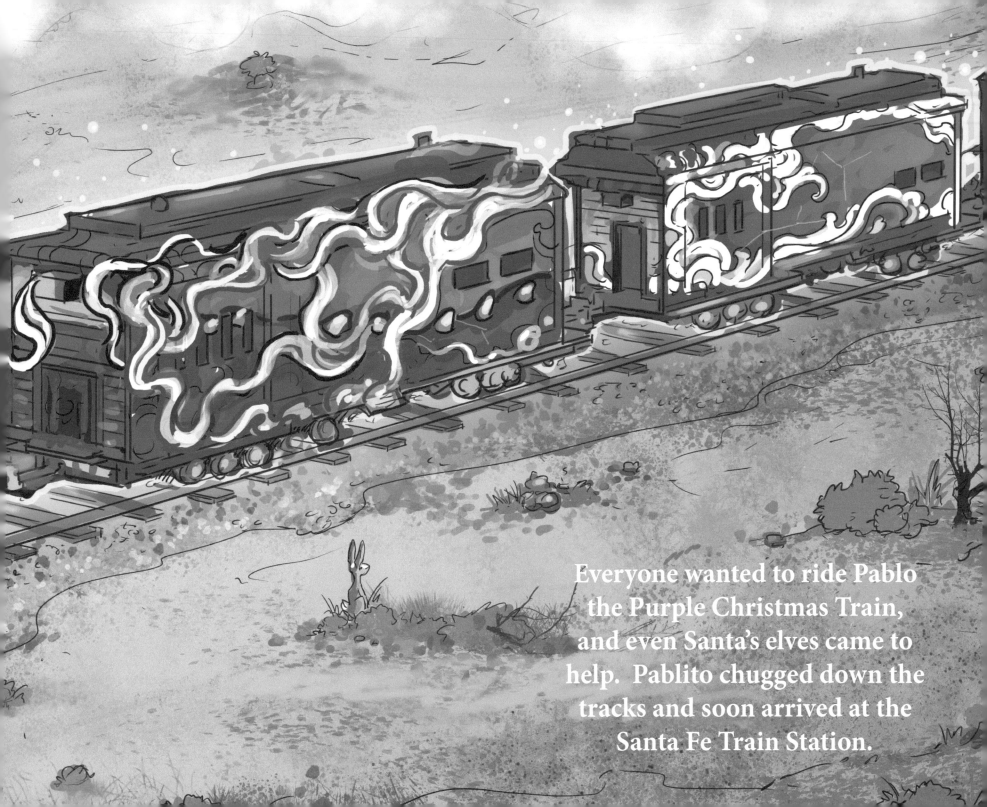

Everyone wanted to ride Pablo
the Purple Christmas Train,
and even Santa's elves came to
help. Pablito chugged down the
tracks and soon arrived at the
Santa Fe Train Station.

The elves unloaded all the
presents and gave them
back to the children who had
gathered there.
That Christmas, the children got
everything they
wanted, and so did the parents—
and even the
grandparents!

All the fun gifts Soggerty had stolen over the years were returned. It was a Christmas surprise no one would ever forget.

When it was all over and the children
had gone home with their presents,
Santa magically transformed Pablito
back into a dragon.

"Pablito, you've done such a good job as the Christmas Train, I want you to help me bring presents and joy to the children of Santa Fe every Christmas Eve. Would you like that?"

"Would I ever!" said Pablito. "But what about the rest of the year? I love being a dragon, but I sure am lonely."

Santa stroked his beard thoughtfully, and then said, "How would you like to come work with me at the North Pole? We could use another dragon up there." Pablito stared at Santa in awe. "You mean there are other dragons at the North Pole?"

Santa roared with laughter. "Ho ho ho!
Of course there are dragons!
There's no wood at the North Pole,
how else do you think we keep warm?
HO HO HO!"

At the North Pole, Pablito met many other dragons and found a new purpose in life, helping Santa and his elves stay toasty warm as they made toys in their workshop. He played and laughed and never had to wish for a friend. He soon made twenty new friends, and they went everywhere together.

They became a thunder of twenty-one.

Now, every year, Pablo the Purple Dragon comes back to New Mexico as Pablo the Purple Christmas Train...

...helping Santa and his elves bring joy
and happiness to the children of Santa Fe
on Christmas Eve.

Pablito is real and still visits the children of Santa Fe every year at Christmas.
Want to ride Pablo the Purple Christmas Train?
Go to skyrailway.com for more information.

(You should probably bring an adult with you so they don't get jealous.
Grown-ups like dragon trains, too.)

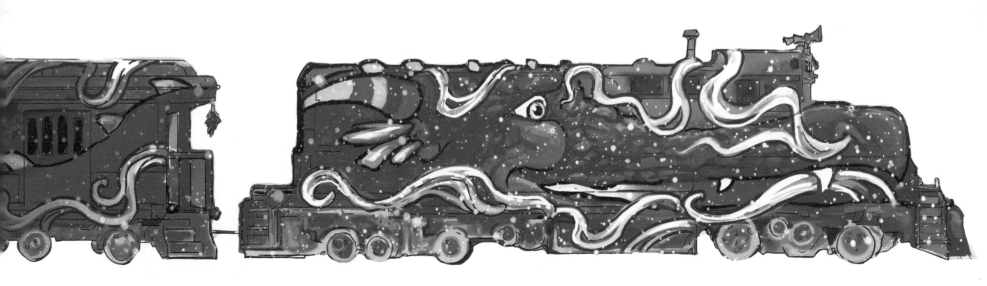

Raya Golden has a unique and stylized vision and brings her work into the world using a variety of mediums ranging from watercolors to digital multi-media. Most recently she completed adapting and inking a 1990s pilot television script entitled STARPORT into a 280-page graphic novel, available through Random House Publishing. She was born in Manhattan, and has slowly made her way across these United States in a steady jaunt westward, finally graduating from the Academy of Art in San Francisco. She currently resides in Santa Fe, New Mexico, with her cat Mr. Boogie.

Douglas Preston has published thirty-six books, both fiction and nonfiction, thirty of which have been *New York Times* bestsellers, several reaching the #1 position. He is the creator, with Lincoln Child, of the famed Pendergast series of thrillers. Several of his books have been made into movies, including *The Jennie Project* (Disney) and *The Relic* (Paramount). Preston currently serves as President of the Authors Guild, the nation's oldest and largest association of authors. While he has been telling stories to children for years, this is the first time he has written one down.

Printed in the USA
CPSIA information can be obtained
at www.ICGtesting.com
LVHW061957281023

761268LV00011B/3